MISANTHROPE

Maryanne Bailer

Contents

ONE

May 16th, 2022

5:30 pm

"Happy Birthday to you" My little brother sang

"Thank you my love" I laughed while planting kisses all over his face

"Alright get out so I can change" I said while kicking him out and locking my door, I Turned around and sigh looking for something to wear and eventually getting frustrated.

"You know what I don't care" I said while plopping down on my bed and getting on my phone, why tf I'm getting hella notifications knowing damn well I don't got no friends

Of course, my fuck ass distant family that only comes around when they need money, telling me happy birthday.

"Yep straight blocking yall cuz I don't know how yall got my shit in the first place" I mumbled

"Obeah" My mom yells

"Bro leave me alone" I mumbled while getting under the cover

"Obeah come here"

"Obeah" She yell while banging on my door "I'm sleep" I yelled

"Open the door" she says I get up and start punching the air oh my fucking gosh

I open the door and I'm met with her ugly ass cheesing and shit "how may I help you" I ask

"I invited some of the neighbors and family over so we can have a get-together for your birthday so I need you to get ready"

I gave her a thumbs-up and slammed my door

Finna fucking kill myself I thought

I look through my closet and dresser searching for an outfit, my phone chimes 3 times making me turn my attention to it to see it's my mom.

Fuck man

I choose a simple outfit and fixed my hair hoping it doesn't rain because somehow each year on my birthday it always finds a way to rain

6:25 pm

I grab my keys and leave out the house and soon as I step out I'm hit with heat and the smell of sex and weed "What in thee actual fuck" I mumble while walking down the steps

It's the fucking the middle of spring and it feels like summer in the Shara desert shit is crazy

I make my way down the block looking around mugging the little kids playing on the sidewalk and ignoring the old folks on they porch saying hi to me

I reach in my purse for my Airpod realizing I forgot them "Fuck" I continue walking zoning out everything around me

Until I finally see the store sorrowed by hella crack heads, drug dealers, sex workers, and, old heads tryna stay cool

I take a deep breath and make my way to the door trying to move quickly so niggas at the door won't say shit to me but just of my luck

"Shawty you can say excuse me" this tall dude says while blocking the door

I look up at him giving him a mug and recognizing him as one of the man thots that I went to high school with

"No, but you can get the fuck outta the way" I say while crossing my arm over my chest

"Say please" ole dude says

"Yeah alright bitch" I said and turned around making my way to another corner store

"mane bring yo ass" ole dude yelled to me

Tuh nawl nigga kiss this ass I thought while turning the corner a decent thing about DC they got a corner store on every corner shit is crazy

I walk down the block a little and reach another corner store not seeing as many people. I'm able to make my way into the store and grab what I came for plus some candy and an Arizona for me shii it ain't my money

I put my stuff on the counter so they can ring my shit up but ain't nobody behind the counter shit ain't nobody at all in this mf except me Niggas bold asf to think I won't walk out the store with ts

"YOOO" I yell

" Somebody come ring my shit up"

Nobody to be found

"Shiiiiiii" I mumble

I take a bag from behind the counter and put my stuff in it and proceed to make my way to the door

Wait nawl fuck that I thought while turning back around and going behind the counter yup I start emptying the cash register cuz I ah be a dumb bitch not to tf I put all the money in another bag then grab me another pack of candy and exit the store

I start making my way back home

6:55 pm

I walk around to the back of my house along with the other people who just arrived smelling the jerked chicken and burgers on the grill and hearing the loud music and everybody laughing and dancing

I'll smack everybody round this bitch ong

"Happy Birthday" Three of my cousins said

Yall fucking stink

I gave them a head nod and smirked at my thoughts and made my way to the house and into the kitchen where my mom and her fuck ass neighborhood friends were chatting it up

"Happy birthday" All her friends said

"yes omg omg happy birthday" my wanna be rich auntie said and came up and hugged me

I gave my mom a look basically telling her to get this bitch off me with my eyes

"Okay okay your cousins and kids your age are in the living room go say hi " my mom said laughing

Yeah ight I gave my mom the stuff she asked for and walked out of the kitchen passing the living room and making my way up stair to my room

I get to my room and see somebody baby laying in my fucking bed

"what in thee actual fuck" I mumble

"yk what I don't even care" I said going to lay down next to it

I put my AirPods in and get on my phone scrolling thru Tik Tok laughing here and there at the videos until I start seeing the thing wake up oh fuck the thing starts to make noise like it was about to cry

I get up and go to the bathroom to wash my hands knowing that imma have to pick it up I sit on my bed picking it up before it starts to make all that unnecessary ass noise

I start rocking it and it smiles at me awe it's kind of cute oh it's a girl look the little bow I thought

I was so caught up in looking at how cute she was I didn't see the man at my doorway

"Oh shit" I said

"Nawl you good" he said

"That's my lor sister I was just coming to check on ha but it seems she good with you she all cheesing and shit"

I chuckled and looked back down at her

"It's a bathroom up here" he asked looking around

"it is..." I mumble

"Can I use it "

"no"

"no?" he asked

"No" I straight faced him

"Why not"

Cuz I said no now get tf out and take the child with you

"Obeah come out back so we can sing you happy birthday" My mom yelled

OHHHH MYYYYY GOOOOOSSSSSHHHH

I got up and handed the baby carefully to the man and walked downstairs and to the back with my mom behind me and headed to the table with people crowding it

There was a purple cake sitting on the table and everybody taking pictures of it and recording it, It was super pretty I love the color purple

I focused my attention on my mom who was counting down for them to sing happy birthday

" 1...2...3 HAPPY BIRT-"

I zoned them out and began looking around to see who all was here I can't even lie they was deep asab in here shii I must be special......hell yeah hell yeah

I saw a lot of the people who stay on the block some family and randoms I spotted the one dude who was by my door but not the baby

"MAKE A WISH"

Oh shit

I closed my eyes

I wish all yall will get the fuck out of my face bitch ass niggas

I smiled and then blew my candles out

"yaaaaay" they all clapped for me like I'm a child all I did was blow out some damn candles damn "alright cut the cake" my mom said

I cut myself a small piece putting it on a plate and turned around but bumped into a nigga chest I looked up and of course it was ole dude from the store

I pushed him out the way and made my way back to my room and locked my door and chilled in there for the rest of the night.

TWO

May 18th

2:31 pm

I walked into my brother's room checking to see what he's up to

"Wyd bub" I asked him

"Fixing my car" he said

While showing me his toy toolbox I laughed at his cuteness and then gave him some candy even though I wasn't supposed to according to my mom but I don't give no fuck

I walked out and made my way downstairs and out the front door I was gonna have a little chill day gonna go get my nails done then go skating

aside from reading and hair that's my favorite thing to do

but first, I need me sum to eat cuz a bitch is starving I pulled up to chickfila and walked inside it blows me every time cuz most places round here don't go a drive-thru so I gotta go inside and be face to face with them people

I order me an 8-piece large fries and a oreo milkshake

I ate my food in the car and then made my way to the nail salon I opened the door the smell of acrylic and nail polish made me smile I love me a fresh set

"Hey how may I help you the lady at the front" asked me

"umm I just want a simple white medium length" I told her

she nodded her head and pointed me over to the waiting area I walked over and sat down waiting for it to be my turn I got on my phone and started to take pictures cuz I felt cute

"Purrr" a little girl looking around 5 said

I chuckled and looked at the person she was with cuz they was burning a hole in my face

Dude with the baby god damn how many kids this nigga got

"Shii wassup nice to see u again" He said while still staring into my soul

"mm" I said while turning my attention back to my phone

"I can take the next person" the lady yelled

I got up and walked to her station telling her what I want and then putting my Airpods in and waiting until she finished

4:42 pm

I made my way to the lady at the front pulling out my card to pay

"Oh no no it's already paid for"

"Huh what you mean" I asked

" He paid for it" she said while pointing to the dude from earlier

"Okay" I mumbled

Why tf-... ykw I don't care free set

I walked out going into my car and put in the direction of the skating rink

I drove a short time and pulled in I made my way to the door that was pulled open quickly before I could get a chance to open

I turned around it's the same nigga..

"Why is you following me" I said while mugging him

"Nawl that's all yo ass" He said mugging me back

" Now go inside fa I close this door on yo gigantic forehead"

"Whole time you not even fun bitch" I said turning around and walking in

"Bitch?" he asks

I ignored him walking to the counter so I can pay to get in

"HI, are you three together or separate" she asked

"Together" he says pushing me to the side

"NIGG-" I was interrupted by the little girl from earlier saying Hi to me I looked at her and gave her a little wave and then turn my attention back to dude

"What size you wear" he asked me

"5 nd a half" I tell the lady she hands me my skates and I handed her my slides I ain't wear no good shoes cuz ain't nobody finna take off with my shii

I head straight into the rink and block everything out

I put my Airpods in because I wasn't finna listen to the white music they was playing I turned my shit all the way up and got into my own vibe

7:34

"Ma where is you at" I said to my mom otp

"Girl I'm out I'll be back tomorrow"

"Ma what... I don't got my key and it's cold" I said growing frustrated

"Go down the street to Mrs.Cooper she got one of my spares" Mrs. cooper was my mom's best friend since birth she a decent lady but talk too fucking much

"Bye" I said hanging up

I thought about it for a little bit then got out of the car making my way down to her house I was finna just sleep in my car but I ain't finna freeze to death nor waste my gas by turning the heat on

Gas is too damn high tuh

I damn near jogged tryna get to her house as fast as I could my ass had on a short sleeve and no jacket

I knocked on her door waiting for her to answer getting annoyed cuz it took her ass longer than 15 second

"Hey baby what you doing in the cold" She said while opening her door fully so I can walk in

I walked in feeling the nice heat "Umm my mom's gone and I forgot my key she said that you might got one"

"Oh okay I'll be right back you can go sit on the couch" she said walking up the steps

Shii nawl I'm good I'll stay my ass right here

"What you doing hea" someone asked scaring me

"Omg" I mumbled

"I'm just saying the stalking gotta stop first you followed me around today then you show up to where I stay shit is crazy" He said laughing

"Watch out I'm not in the mood" I tell him

"Why"

"Somebody did you sum?"

I shook my head and looked at the stairs growing impatient at the fact that Mrs. Cooper was taking forever

"what yo name is?"

"Why are you worried" I said mugging him

He mugged me back

"Imma ask you again....what's yo name"

I chuckled cuz who tf..."What's yo name all worried bout me fa what"

" My name Ziyaan"

" Now tell me your" He said while licking his lips

"Obeah" I said while now making eye contact with him

Not he actually kinda fine

He smiled at me making me scrunch up my eyebrows

I ain't say that out loud did I..?

" Okay found it" Mrs. coopers said while coming down the steps

I turned my attention to her

"thanks" I said taking the key from her "bye" I said leaving out and making sure to slam it

I love slamming doors makes me feel like a white boy that just said fuck you mom

I started to make my way back to my house but stopped when I heard my name getting called

"What Ziyaan" I said with an attitude

"I just wanna get yo number" he said showing his pearly whites

"No fuck out my face" I continued to walk to my house I heard his footsteps behind me but ignored em

I walked up the steps of my house and turned to face him

"Why youn gotta password on yo phone" He asked

I scrunched my face up realizing he had my shit in his hands

Yep that's my cue

I swung but he weaved my shit making me get mad

"chill" he said grabbing both my hands

"Get the fuck offa me" I said yelling

"Calm yo dumb ass down"

He let me go putting me against the door and snatchin the key outta my hand

"Bro what the fuck is you on" I yelled

"You yelling fa what tho" He said mugging me and opening the door

" Nigga get the fuc-"

"Shut up" he said pushing me inside and catching me before I could fall

how you gone push me then catch me...

I reached into my purse getting my pocket knife

"Get the fuck out bro" I pointed the knife at him

"Chill" he smirked at me and handed me my phone back

"Answer when I call and lock the door" He closed the door

Bro wtf just happened I hurried up and locked the door and made sure to turn the security system on

I went up stair and into the bathroom hoping that a bath would calm my nerves my heart was racing but I wasn't scared I don't know what the fuck..

I turned on the water letting the tub fill up and putting bubbles in I turned some music on and got in my body relaxed as soon as I felt the warm water hit my toes I got comfortable and relaxed vibing to the music

There's really no end, there's really no beginningThere's really no real, there's really no pretendingThere's really no fail, there's really no winning'Cause nothing really isn't, everything really isn't

I sang lowly as the song came to an end the next song began to start but was cut off by my phone ringing Unkown it read I declined and unpaused my music but my phone rung yet again

I answered covering the camera because whoever it was called me ft

"speak" I said

"Yoo" Ziyaan said putting his face in the camera

"What nigga I'm in the bath" I said

"Oh shit my bad carry on act like I'm not here"

You know what I don't care I grabbed my speaker connecting it to my phone so my music can be louder since it was low now that I'm otp

I pressed play on my music

I hummed lowly to While Were Young by Jhene Aiko

I got back in my vibe

We should just do whatever we want and tell everyone that we fell in love with each other Ooh that we found the one in one another

I sang softly

I'm tellin' everybody you're mine and I like it, I like itAnd I really hope you don't mind, I can't fight it

Ziyaan sang lowly I chuckled at him tryna sing like he was good we continued to vibe like that until I got out of my bath

THREE

June 3rd

1:28 PM

"Bro shut the fuck up" I said smacking Mal

"Cuz you ain't have to hit me that hard" he said getting into a fighting stance

I mugged him and walked across the street and dapped up the niggas playing dice

"Hop in" Ricky said reaching for a lighter

"Inna lor bit"

I looked around checking my surroundings everybody was out this bitch today

" Whats the moves today" i asked knowing somebody had to be having a party

"Shii we shutting down the whole block today everybody rey come round this bitch at 6"

"mmm" i hummed while noding my head

I sat down on the curb getting on my phone checking to see who texted me

I laughed at how happy her lor ass was about the ice cream truck I got up making my way over to her house me and her been vibing these past couple of days on some friendly shii

she cool when she not cussing me out

I laughed watching her damn near almost falling down the steps tryna get out here

"Where the fuck it's at" She asked looking around

"Nawl what the fuck is you wearing" I asked now mugging the fuck outta her

---

2:01 PM

" Oh this" I asked smirking

I did a little spin then started shaking my ass cuz a bitch looked good I turned around to look at him and laughed at his facial expression

"I don't look good" I said standing straight up with my arms crossed

"Where you boutta go obeah"

"Ummmm anywho where the ice cream truck at" I pouting

" I ain't just ask you sum"

I snapped my neck toward him

"BOO the fuck I'm grown"I said now mugging the fuck outta him

"mmm" he hummed

I looked around finally finding the ice cream truck and making my way toward it but stopped once I saw it pull off

I know you fucking lying

"That's what the fuck yo ass get" I heard Zi say from behind me

"Oh my fucking gosh I would of fucking made it if yo ass wasn't bitchin at me for like 4 mins" I huffed

oops...bitch run

I started speed-walking away but quickly was pulled back

uh oh guess imma have to fight this nigga today

"Obeah why you tryna start with me" he said in my ear

Ouuu don't do that gone get sum started

"Zi move" I said trying to hold my smile in

"Yo mom home" he asked

"noo" I said turning to face him

"Come on"

We walked into my house and made our way to my room closing the door behind us

"You needa change" He said while pressing his body against mine and pulling my bathing suit top down so my under boob wasn't showing

"Whyy" I looked up at him

He looked down at me and we made eye contact

"Cuz I said" he leaned in closer to my face

"Bring me to my closet" I said putting my arms up so he can pick me up

Compared to him I was tiny asl but that ain't mean shii cuz ill still whoop him and he knows that

He picked me up making me wrap my arms around his neck and legs around his waisted and walked me to my closet

I got a plain white crop top and showed it to him for his approval

I can't believe I'm actually changing for this nigga

I put the shirt on over the top I already had on and then we laid on my bed

"You tryna smoke" he asked

Duhhh nigga

I nodded my head

I watched as he took the prerolled blunt from behind his ear and got out a lighter lighting the blunt then doing a deep in heal and passing it off to me

he got comfortable on my bed laying flat out and pulled me on his lap

we stayed in that position while taking turns hitting the blunt

---

3:28 Pm

Them^

"What is thaaaaat" Beah laughed

"That's how you do it" Zi laughed tryna do the Tik Tok dance

"No the fuck its not"

"Get up and show me then" Zi pulled Beah off the bed

"Unt unt my hip bad" She laughed

"Nawl you lame" ZI lay back on the bed

Beah jumped on top of him laughing

"Noooo I'm not"

she got on his lap straddling him

"mmmhmm" he hummed

they looked at each other

"You gone come with me to the block party" Zi asked while sliding his hand in Beah's pants and resting them on her butt

"Unt unt too many people"

"Fuck them they ain't gone do you nun"

"I knooow but still" Beah whined

she began moving back and forth making him groan the high was making them both extremely horny but neither wanted to give in

So they were playing cat and mouse

"mmmmm chill out" Zi groaned

"what I'm doing " she smirked

He bit his lip rubbing her butt

"Gimmie kiss" Zi said

Without hesitation, Beah leaned in and they locked lips having a battle to see who will pull away first

"Mmm" they both moaned when pulling away from the kiss

"Come on fa I fuck the shit outta you" Zi got up with Beah still wrapped around him

"where are we going" Beah laughed

6:56 pm

"Spray me with ts and imma beat yo ass" I yelled

Everybody was out this bitch the grill was going, water balloon and water gun fighting, music, ice cream, shii mfs had a whole slipping slide going down the whole block

The vibes was good asl right now everybody was laughing and smiling

"You soooo lame it's just water" Beah yelled to me over the loud music

"I don't give a fuck Keshia" I yelled back

"Ewwww you so corny" she walked closer to me

I laughed

"Come on I don't know who told you to dress all cute" She whined

"Ight cry baby damn shut up"

"Nigga fuck you" I watched as she took off her top revealing the same top she had on earlier

Really should beat ha ass for having her titties out but she looks good imma let it slide

She took her pants off leaving her in her bathing suit bottom

Ouuu shii my dick hard

"Come on" She took my shirt and jacket off for me throwing them to the side

"What you got on under these" She tugged on my jeans

"Shii nun less you want me in my drawls"

She mugged making me chuckle

She dragged me up to the slip-in slide making me sit down first and her on my lap we went down and that shit hurt like a mutha fucka had me thinking I got rug burn

"less go again" she said in excitement

"Ba- that shit hurt" I said mugging her

"Noooo it didn't" she said

"Yes the fuck it did you ain't feel nun of the shit because you was on top of me"

"You a big baby" She said putting her hands up so I can pick her up

I picked her up

"But you the one that's getting carried like one"

"And what about it" She rested her head on my shoulder

"What's wrong" I asked

"I'm tired and these people keep looking at me like I won't beat they ass"

"Cuz you fine asf"

"Stooop"

"Not I got you blushing" I teased

"Yaan" Mal called out to me

"What it is" I dapped him up

"This you" He pointed to Beah

"Why are you worried" Beah mugged

"Shii my bad" He said putting his hands up in defense

"But yaan I was tryna see if you gone slide with me to CeCe house ha sister rey be there" He said

"Shii I'll let you know" I said

"Bring me in the house" Beah whispered in my ear

"Ight imma hit you later" I told mal

8:54 PM

"What you still here fa" I asked Zi

I had just gotten out of the shower and expected him to leave once I got in

"Damn I can't chill here" He asked

"Oh I was expecting you to go to CeCe's house"

And fuck on her sister

"Don't nobody want that bitch" He fussed

I ignored him going to my closet to find my ugg slides

"I meaaaan you can go now" I said laying in my bed and turning on the tv

"Ight bra" He said slamming my door

Bitch ass nigga

I got on Netflix and putting on Ozark I ended up falling asleep to that

FOUR

June 4th

2:25 AM

I reached for my phone to check the time

"Ughh" I groaned

I got up going to the bathroom then laying back down

What is that sound

Ain't no way this nigga...

I chuckled

"Zi get the fuck up" I said kicking him

When Zi had left earlier he went home to shower and change then came back to Obeah's house

He ain't wanna wake her up so he lay on the floor and end up falling asleep there

"Oh shit" He said wiping the drool off his face

"You was sleeping good huh" I laughed

"Yeah and you needa learn to lock the damn door or somebody gone take off with yo shit"

"Oop I forgot" I covered her mouth

"mmm" Zi hummed getting up and laying next to me

"I woke you up" he asked

"No it was just random"

I grabbed the remote looking for something to watch

"Netflix been down bad man" I mumbled

Zi pulled me back and making me small spoon

I grabbed my covers putting it over both of us and getting comfortable I switched apps going on to Hulu turning on Bob's Burgers

I love Bob's burgers idc idc~Liaa

I watched for a little then ended up falling asleep right after Zi

1:54 PM

"Man you taking too long" Zi said getting irritated

"Shut up damn" I said walking out of my closet

"You straight ugly tryna match me" Zi laughed

"You know what never mind" I said boutta go back into my closet

"Shut up and bring yo ass"He dragged me down the stairs

I locked the front door and then hurried up to the passenger's side

"Why the fuck I gotta drive" Zi complained

"Cuz ion want too" I connected my phone to the aux

"Nawl the disrespect is crazy you force me to drive and listen to your shitty ass music" Zi said shaking his head

"NIgga BOO cuz nun bout my music shitty dirt neck"

He laughed pulling out

I played Losing my cool by Rod wave making sure to turn it all the way up life of a youngin Tryna balance my pain became my struggleI was already deep off in my thoughts, and feelin funnyHow the ones that I love the most just can't keep it a hunnid?I never thought I'd get this far, I used to doubt myself

I sang while hitting Zi's chest

"Man why u can't sing like a normal person hitting on me n shii" he complained

"Shut uuuuuup damn"

They told me 10 at 14, I went and found myselfIn my cell writin' raps, often thinkin' 'bout DejaBefore she died, I told her my dreams and my aspirationsI used to cry just thinkin' 'bout all the shit she was facin'I know she smilin' lookin' down 'cause I finally done made it

I continued to sing while holding my chest

I love my lil' brother, he feel like big brother be trippin'That shit just make me so damn mad that he don't fuckin' listenAnd my big brother really gifted, but he really trippin'He tell me him and his addictionAin't none of my business In his brain, he rock star livin'Yeah, and we was raised the same, but we way different Either way and if you right or wrong, I'm forever with you

"Hol up Hol up this my part" I screamed and turning it up more

Gotta watch my back 'cause I don't trust these hoes or trust these niggas Tell me, who can you trust when people so deceivin'? Don't want no love 'cause she gon' leave, and come back when she need meShe lookin' dead in my eyes, lyin' like a demonHow you slap the hand that had fed you, bite the hand that feed you?I don't get it neither, yeah, yeahI don't get it neitherMy family don't see Nuni, they see Rod Wave So mentally and physically, I stay far away

"Oh my fucking gosh that man is too fye bro" I said tryna catch my breath

If you don't like rod your dead smoking dick!!!~Liaa

"He ight" Zi hating ass said

I rolled my eyes

I'm hungry asab

"What you wanna eat" He asked

"Ight na cuz that's like yo 3rd time reading my mind" I mugged him

He chuckled pulling into the mall parking lot

He parked and then came to my side opening my door for me

2:23 PM

"Man I'm finna let yo ass starve if you don't hurry up and choose sum" Zi complained

"I don't know what I want" I whined

"Ouuuu I want a Cinnamon Pretzel" I ran to Aunt Annie

I'm pretty sure Aunt Annies is a DMV thing but if you come down here you gotta try it shii is too good!~ Liaa

Zi came behind me pressing up against me

Ouuuu baby and that's just on soft lemme find out

"Order yo shii man" He chuckled

"Lemme get the cinnamon pretzel bites and a pink lemonade" I order

"9.78" The girl said eyeing Zi

She must got a wandering eye

She must Zi said in my head

I turned around to look at him and he smiled at me

"Hea" The girl said popping her gum

"I hope you choke on that shit " I said grabbing my stuff

Zi busted out laughing

We sat down so I can eat my stuff then began walking around

"Mall bout dry asab " Zi said

"I swear" I walked into Coach

"Let's take a picture" I smiled

"Ight" Zi said

"Excuse me can you take our picture" he asked this older lady

2:55 PM

"So you telling me you choosing Rod wave over Nocap" Zi asked

"Yes nigga any day the fuck" Beah laughed

"You geeking" Zi pushed Beah

"We not cool no more"

"Look Nocap fye but ROD is a different level so not too fucking much" Beah pointed her finger in his face

Zi laughed

"What's yo favorite color" Beah asked

"Black, I already know yo shit purple by yo room"

"Yeah purple and baby blue"

"How many siblings you got" Zi asked wrapping his arm around her shoulder

"I got two, My brother and sister"

Zi scrunched his eyebrows up "How come ion never see em"

"Cuz my sister stay in NC for school and my brother always with my mom and as you can see my mama love to go out" She stated

"What about you" She looked up at him

Zi shook his head"I got 7 shii might got more for all I know"

"God damn" Beah covered her mouth

Zi chuckled "Ion really talk to half of them only the ones from my mom's side"

"How many yo mom got" She questioned

"She got three you already saw two of em" He said

"The baby and little girl at the nail salon" She asked

"Yeah Zamiyah and Zariyah"

"Awwwe all yall got Z's that's so cute"

"Man shut the fuck up" ZI laughed

"Zi, when's your birthday" She asked

"July 4th"

"Ouu you must feel special" Beah laughed

"Imma go into foot locker then we can go" Zi walked into the foot locker

"Ouu" Beah went over nd picking up some Oreo 4s

"Yo ass lucky yo feet small cuz us big feet people don't get that lucky" Zi huffed

Zi Picked up some hoodies then they went to check out

"I can pay for my shoes" Beah said

"Man move" Zi moved Beah to the side and paid for everything

He grab the bags and they left out the store

Beah gave Zi a side stare

"What" Zi said

Beah rolled her eye "Nun"

"Come here" ZI chuckled

He picked her up making her smile and they made their way to the car

"You wanna go to the college football game later" Zi asked turning the car on

"uh I'll think about it"

"Huh you said that you coming...oh okay ill be in front of yo house at 7"

6:45 PM

"This Bipolar ass weather" I mumbled

I drove down the street and pulled into Beah's driveway I honked my horn so she could hurry up

10 mins later her ass finally came out

"Heyy" She cheesed

I chuckled " I can't even cuss you out yo ass look too good"

"Thank you" She kissed my cheek

I grabbed her neck pulling her into an actually kiss

" I don't know what the fuck you thought this was" I said pulling away

"Unt unt cuz you getting too comfortable kissing me" She side-eyed me

"ion see the problem"I backed out

"I don't know where the fuck yo lips been at" She mugged

"Gone somewhere with that" I mugged her back

We drove talking about dumb shii then pulled into the parking lot and started walking to the game which was packed

"Wait take my picture" She handed me her phone

I smiled watching her do her lor dance

She laughed "Ight come on"

I handed her, her phone back and then we found our seats

"See ion like this" Beah sat down

"What nun even happened"

"It's too many people make me feel uncomfortable"

"Just chill"I pulled her on top of my lap

We watched the game until it was the end of 2nd quarter then things started to get messy

"Get up" I tapped Beah's leg

Bro I know that's not Mal

Mal is like my hot head lor brother so shii I'm ready to go to war fa him whenever and I knew my eyes weren't deceiving me and it look like they was tryna jump him

I ran down to where they was at

"What it is" I asked mel

7:48 PM

I ran out the parking lot of the college and turned the block

I don't know what happened but all I know is I heard shooting and got the fuck from outta there

I continue walking in the direction of my house with my flash on it was dark asab out hea got me feeling somebody gone snatch me up

Oh shii

I texted Zi to make sure he was good cuz I most definitely just dipped and didn't even check for him

But shii everyone for them self stinka

I damn near almost dropped my phone once I heard screaming from behind me

OH FUCK NO

I ran in the direction of my house not looking back

Once I made it I hurried up and got inside locking the door

"what's wrong with you" my mom asked from behind me

Making me jump "OH SHIT" I screamed grabbing my chest

"You almost made me shit myself " I said tryna catch my breath

"Girl you the one coming in here like you don't got no sense" She walked up the stair

I shook my head then made my way to my room

FIVE

June 23rd

1:40 PM

"I KNOW THAT AIN'T MY FINE ASS SISTER" I yelled

My sister finally came home from college and I'm so hyped she is hands down my favorite person and I only got two of those

"Bitch I missed you" She ran hugging me

"I missed you moreeee" I hugged her back tightly

"Ouu hol up bitch you look good" She played with my hair

"Yup ate the girly's up with pink" I laughed

"Lemme go put my shii down cuz I got so much shii to tell you bout" She ran upstairs to her room

I went into the living room laying down on the couch and got on Instagram I clicked on Zi's story

We ain't talked since June 8th I'm guessing cuz after that football game I told him I ain't really with the fighting, drugs, and shooting

Shii it might not seem like it but I value my life and ts is one of the quickest ways to get you killed

But anywho I guess that made him distance himself but ask me if I give af

410.Zi 10mins ago

Send message

That's them just use your imagination!! ~Liaa

I laughed at the video and then responded with a laughing emoji

"What got you cheesing that hard" Oliva said trying to look at my phone

"Bitch boo mind yo business" I turned my phone off

She gave me a side eye" Bitch lemme find out" she said sitting next to me

I smiled "But anywho what's been going on"

" Girlll so first a bitch almost done with school FINALLY" She laughed

"So proud of you" I jumped on her

"Bitch you too damn big" She pushed me

"Ight fuck you too" I put my middle finger up

She laughed "Oou bitch and guess what"

I scrunched my eyebrows

"I got me some rich dick" She stuck her tongue

"WAAAAAAIIIITTTTT" I looked at her shocked

"Since fucking when " I asked

"Like 4 months now" She laughed

"You just now telling me oh mk I see how it is" I said rolling my eyes at her

"Don't do me cuz what the fuck you been doing" She smirked at me

"Ion know what you talking bout" I drunk juice

"Oh okay yeah cuz I most def ain't see an arm around you when we was on ft that one day or wait that one video of yall at the block part when some dude was carrying yo ass" She said

I know this hoe ain't talk bout me and Zi

my jaw dropped "Hol the fuck on what video" I laughed

"mmmm" She hummed taking her phone out

"This not you " She put her phone in my face

"Who posted that" I frowned

See one thing ion like is somebody in my business the fuck

"Girl yall in the 202 shade room" She chuckled

I kissed my teeth "People are weird"

"Put who is he" she asked

"Nobody" I mumbled

"Ight imma leave you alone bout it but you know imma ask you again later" She got up

"Let go live" she smiled

"Yuhhh and shake some ass" I smirked

"See my nigga ah beat my ass" she said starting the live

"Bitches get a nigga and don't know how to act" I laughed

"YUP" she popped her P setting the phone up

"Hol up I needa find some music to shake to" I stuck my tongue out

"Why somebody tryna play with you all like you got nun to shake"She snapped her head towards me

"Who don't...shii it might now be much but this mf move TUH" I said

"MATTER FACT DJ DROP THAT BEAT" I yelled

This hoe started to sing wine slow

I looked at her like she was dumb like this hoe could've song anything else

"wait you know what you gone make my Jamaican come out" I laughed

I set the phone up nd began to wine to her singing

ouu shii I said getting up "why you ain't tell me to stretch"

I plopped down on the couch

4:40 PM

"Uhh how may I help you" I said to Zi and Ole dude from the block party

"You look good" ZI said licking his lips

I smiled "Thank you Zi what you and yo little friend knocking at my door for"

"My name Mal" he put his hand out so I can dap him up

"Unt unt for all I know yo hand could've been in yo ass like 2 mins ago" I mugged

"Man see I told you this girl bout mean as hell for no reason" He huffed

"Tuh cuz you ain't seen mean yet" I put my hands on my hips

"Man yall shut the fuck up I came cuz I missed you and yo ass out hea geekin"He said pushing me aside and walking in

Gone walk in here like he owns the place nigga boo tf

He turned around and mugged me

"What" I mugged back

He shook his head and walked into the living room

"Oh shit wassup sister in law" he said dapping up Olivia

"Who getting married" I scrunched my eyebrows up

"Yall" Mal pointed to me and Zi

"Yall hilarious and I enjoyed the show but yall can get the fuck out now" I said plopping down on the couch

"This how you treat yo brother in law and husband" Mal asked holding his chest

Olivia busted out laughing

"Lord help me" I mumbled

"Let's watch a movie" Zi plopped down next to me

"We gotta watch that black phone joint"Mal sat down on the other side of me

bro after I watched that shii I had a dream that i was in that nigga basement man i woke up cheeks clenched tf up~Liaa

Zi wrapped his arms around me then pulled the blanket over us two

He leaned in and whispered in my ear "Obeah I missed you yk"

"Mmm" I hummed

"My bad for just dipping out on you I was just tryna figure some things out" He whispered in my ear

"It's okay i guess" I mumbled playing with his finger

"Imma talk to you later ight" He kissed my forehead

I rested my head on his shoulder "Ight"

"I like this pink on you ngl" He touched my hair

"Thank you" I smiled

"Yall ugly" Olivia said cheesing

"Shut up hoe" I mugged

"found it" Mal announced clicking on the movie

"Unt Unt that look scary ion like scary movies" I raised my eyebrows

"Oh shut up cry baby" Zi chuckled

I flicked him off

"Wait don't start yet yall want popcorn" I asked

Not me being nice fuck yall

I went to the kitchen and popped enough for all of them and got a couple packs of candy

And we started the movie

8:21 PM

"Wake yo ass up" I whispered to Beah picking her up bridal style

All these nigga fell asleep during the movie

"Hmm" she hummed wrapping her arms around my neck

I brought her upstairs into her room and then threw her on the bed

"Cuz what the fuck was the reason" she straight-faced me

" I fucking missed you" I jumped on her

"You too fucking heavy" she yelled

"Shut up" I laughed

"But you the one who left" She shrugged

"I know I listened to what you said and I'm tryna get somethings straight for you I really like yo ass and wanna be with you" I said

She smiled "Awwe Zi forreal"

"Yeah" I chuckled

"I like you but you ain't have to just leave me" She rolled her eyes

"I know I apologize for that it ain't gone happen again" I reassured her

"Thank you Zi" She hugged me tight

I hugged her back "Fa what ma"

"Being there I done got so comfortable in this little bit of time I've known you it crazy asl to me" She admitted

I smiled

"Stop" She laughed getting up

"Where you going" I pulled her onto my lap

"Zi we just left them downstairs we not going back down there" she asked

"Man fuck them" I mugged

"You look so good" I licked my lips

"mmm you look fine asl" She grinded back and forth on my hard dick

She pulled me into a kiss

I slid my hands into her shorts playing with her clit thru her panties causing her to pull away from the kiss and let out a soft moan

I flipped us over and took her shorts and panties off

I wasted no time sliding two fingers into her wet pussy making her gasp for air

I started off slow giving her some time to adjust then sped my pace up

"slow down" she moaned

I sped my pace up making her moan louder

"Can I taste you ma" I asked

"Mm yes baby" she moaned

I bent down sucking and kissing her clit

"oh fuck Zi" she moaned throwing her head back

"Look at me" I demanded

We made eye contact as I aggressively ate her up and pumped my fingers in and out of her pussy

"mmm I'm finna Oh my- cummm" She moaned

"let it out" I said hitting her spot

"Wait ohh i-its n-ot c-" She squirted all over my face

"Ouu shit" I smiled

I took my fingers out and slurped all her juices up

"Mmmm" she moaned softly

"Fuck you taste so good" I stood up looking down at her

"Thank you" she said shyly hiding her face

I chuckled "Don't be acting all shy now like you ain't just squirt all over my face" I walked into the bathroom wiping my face

"Stop that so embarrassing" She pouted

I leaned down kissing her making sure she tasted herself

She untied my sweat pants and started to play with my dick

she pulled away from the kiss "I want some" she bit her lip

"You not even ready for all that" i moved her hand

"please" she whinned

I shook my head and kissed her forehead then picked her up bringing her to the bathroom getting a bath for both of us ready

SIX

June 24th

11:23 AM

"You think they heard us?"

"yeah they heard yo ass you was like omg ziiiiii" Zi mocked me

"Ziyaan" I hit him in his chest

"You know I ain't lying" he laughed

I pouted "it's not funny"

"Oh shut up lor baby" he plucked my forehead

"I'm hungry come on" I pulled him down the stairs

we walked into the kitchen running into Oliva and Mal

"Hey.......How yall doing" I scratched my head

"mmmm" both of them hummed

"What" I giggled looking into the fridge

I searched the fridge for some bacon and eggs, I turned around and they all looked away acting like they wasn't looking at me

"Fucking creeps I'll be wrong if I throw an egg at each yall forehead the fuck" I mugged them

"Can you make me sum please" Olivia poked her lip out

I chuckled "Bitch you look fucking dumb and no I ain't making nun of yall shit"

"How you open this" Mal picked up an egg

"Nigga crack it onna counter" Zi said

He banged it on the counter making the egg break and fall all over the floor

I scratched my head"Bro ain't no wa-"

"This nigga" Zi walked away

"How the fuck you ev-" Olivia scrunched her eyebrows up

"That ain't even my fault I did what I was told" he started cleaning the egg up

"Niggas ain't neva cracked an egg" Olivia asked

Making mal shake his head no

"Lemme have this" Zi took my Juice box out of the fridge

"Absolutely not" I snatched it from him

"Greedy" He mumbled

"How bout all yall get the fuck out yall making me hot" I mugged them all

"We hungry too I understand you not making them breakfast but what about me yo husband" Zi pointed to himself

"It's cereal right there" I pointed to the pantry

"Wooooow" They all said

"I hate yall" I said putting the bacon in the oven

"Come make yall own shii" I huffed

"But you just told us to get out bitch make up yo mind" Oliva laughed

"Shut up" I threw the juice box at her head

"Yall got frozen waffles I know how to make those" Mal looked in the freezer

"I bet you fucking do"Zi laughed

"Beah how I roll this" Olivia asked holding the croissants you have to bake

I ignored her mixing my eggs and adding seasoning

I hate some plan eggs like that salt and pepper ain't gone do it for me add some garlic power or sum damn ~LIaa

I put the eggs in the pan scrabbling them, then taking them out I continued doing what I was doing not paying them no mind

I took my bacon out and put two waffle inna toaster

Told these pussy niggas not to fuck with usAnd shout out to the hoes they be suckin us I rapped in my head

See now I gotta play that song

"Hey Alexa play cutting up" I yelled

290 shit man, out west shit niggaYou know how we rockin niggaGet yo guns up get yo funds upYou On That Opp Shit, Get Mob Stick BitchStraight Gang Shit, Aye, Boochie Gang

Blasted through the speaker

"Oh hell nawl it's too early Alexa pause the music" Olivia yelled

She ain't just...

"Alexa unpause" I said calmly

AyeShe said she like my swag, I be cuttin' upHe can't hang with us cause he ain't cut enough You don't want war with us, you ain't tough enough I just bought a 5th of Henny and I drunk it up BITCH!

I rapped loudly while putting butter on my waffles I zoned them out. bitch it's neva too early for lud foe

5:20 PM

"Oh look who is finally back" I announced while opening the door for my mom

"where Olivia" she walked in not paying me no mind

Well fuck you too

Zi and Mal left so it was just me and Olivia chilling she ran and gave Olivia a hug

"Umm where Mari" I asked referring to my brother

"with his dad" She turned to look at me

I rolled my eyes I truly hate that nigga he's like 40 sum still at his mama's house and his breath stank

I made my way upstairs cuz now all the fun was over since my mom was back

I texted Zi to see what he was doing then went on Instagram scrolling thru my feed and stopped once I got a dm

I clicked on it seeing it was from my sister it was a post promoting a party for later that was near us

I texted back a thumbs down because this hoe alr know ion do party too many fucking people makes me sick

Incoming Facetime from ZI my AirPods read

I answer putting my face in the camera

"Helloo" I said

"Imma come to get you inna lor bit" he said

"Okay where you at right now" I asked

"I'm in Park heights" He responded

"Why the hell you in Baltimore" I raised my eyebrows

"I'm visiting my peoples" he laughed

"Ohhh okay I'm finna go get ready" I said getting up

"ight later" He said

"Later be safe" I hung up

I walk into the closet looking for something to wear

"wait I don't even know where he taking me" I mumbled

I texted him asking if should I dress up and he responded with a yes

Mmmmmk let's see I could go with pink to match my hair.......mm kinda tacky

Wear white you'll look good in that I heard Zi's voice in my head

"I swear I be around this nigga too much hear his voice and shii" I mumbled picking out a white skirt

7:34 PM

"Nawl cuz you took mad lon-" I stopped mid-sentence once I saw Zi standing there with some flowers

"Is that for meee" I smiled walking towards him

He chuckled "Yes baby" he handed me the flowers

"Awwwe Zi" I hugged him

He hugged me back "and my bad for taking long"

He opened the door for me and i got into the car closing the door

"These are so pretty" I admired the flowers

He reached over grabbed the seat belt and buckled it for me

"Thank you husband" I kissed his cheek

They uglyyyyy ~Liaa

He pulled out of the driveway
"you got everything" He asked
"Yeah" I said and he pulled off
We shortly arrived and hopped out the car
"Lemme take yo picture" Zi pulled his phone out
"I was gone ask you anyway" I laughed
@ itsbeah

Liked by 410.Zi and 12,842 others

itsbeah Colorful hair don't care!

view all 4,031 comments

"you look so beautiful" Zi said opening the door for me

"Thank you my love" I walked in

"Hello do yall have a reservation" the lady greeted us

"yeah for 8" Zi responded

"Okay come this way" we followed behind her and took our seats

"Someone will be here shortly to take your order" She gave us our menus

we both gave her a nod

"How was your day" I asked

"It was coo..." He trailed off

I raised my eyebrows and looked up at him seeing he was deep into his phone

"mmm" I hummed looking down at the menu

he lifted my head up making eye contact with me

"How was your day ma" he tilted his head

"it was boring" I mumble

"What you do down in Baltimore" I added

he twisted his lip "I had to make a couple of sales and visit some family"

"Are you gonna leave the..." I stopped mid-sentence

"Hmm" he raised his eyebrows

"Well before I ask you that what's your reason for begin involved with the drug business" I bit my lip

"Well I ain't from the best part of Baltimore so it wasn't that many choices for me school system was ass I was hoping basketball would get me somewhere but they ain't take me serious cuz of where I was from" He sat up looking directly into my eyes

"awwe Zi, do you still play basketball" I asked

"Yeah whenever I got the time" he said

"But as I was gonna say before are you planning on leaving all that" I spoke

I watched as his facial expression changed making me raise my eyebrows

"ion know" He said nonchalantly

I took a deep breath "What do you mean you don't know"

"I mean that's how I get my money... shii the streets is all I know" He shrugged

I shook my head showing my disappointment and looked back down at the menu

it was complete silence between us until the waiter came

"Hello, can I get you guys started with drink" She asked

"a pink lemonade" I told the lady

she looked at Zi and he got the same thing and we ordered our food

8:29 PM

"Obeah" I spoke sternly

She looked up at me showing me that she was listening

I rubbed my hands down my face "Ight look I wanted to go out with you before i left t-"

"Hol up" she stopped me mid-sentence

"Your leaving bro... we ain't talk for like 2 weeks you came back just leave again" She mugged

"Beah look it ain't even like that if I could i would stay with you" I expressed

"How long are you leaving and where are you going" she questioned

" A week or two..." I said

"I asked you two questions" she crossed her arms

"Ayy look that's all i can tell you" I spoked

"Tuh okay" she chuckled

I sighed "Look ion want you thinking nun bad " I said getting frustrated

I alr knew me telling Beah that I was leaving was gone make her feel some typa way but it wasn't nun I could do about it

We sat in silence once again eating our food

9:45 PM

"Bye Beah" I said

She slammed the car door and I watched her walk into the house and then pulled off

SEVEN

June 24th

11:32 PM

"Beah you really just gone block him" Olivia asked

"Yes I'm not rey get attached and then get hurt" I laid down

She thinks I'm doing too much but I know myself. Soon as I got home I got to overthinking it took me a while to make peace with my overthinking but now here I am once again...

Overthinking deadass ruins you bro...

"omg" I started hitting my pillow

"I will go find him right now and whoop him" she said

"Got my sis in her feeling and shii" she added

"Ight now cuz I ain't in my feeling " I side-eyed her

she side-eyed me back "if you say so"

we both laughed

She got on her laptop and I stared at the ceiling just thinking

"Beah" she tapped me

"Ain't his name Ziyaan Zypar Orabás" she asked

"Yeah, why..." I looked at her

"Well first bitch that demonic ass name and uh bitch do he got a twin brother or sum" She raised her eyebrow

"Not that I know of" I sat up

"well it's multiple reports saying Teen Shot and Killed in Park Heights Baltimore and umm it's most definitely Zi" she scratched her head

"Olivia" I straight-faced her

"I'm so serious Beah but all these reports are from 2019" She raised her eyebrow

"Get the fuck on" I chuckled

"BITCH look for your damn self" she gave me her computer

I scrolled thru it seeing that the person indeed looked like Zi and she did put his full name into the google search

"what the fuck this don't make no sense" I handed her back her computer

I grabbed my phone and unblocked him

"Bitch I'm finna text him" I mumbled

"Just say hey" she said

I texted him Hey and asked what he was doing

"Lemme see" I took her computer back

I retyped his name to see if maybe she got something wrong but got the same thing I scrolled down and click on his Instagram to see it was the same one that I followed

"last active October 14, 2019" I read out loud

But how

I clicked on his most recent post and saw it was from June 2019 I grabbed my phone and went to his Instagram from off my account I clicked on his most recent and it was from 2 days ago

"Brooo what the fuck" I huffed

"Search this Instagram acc on yo phone" I told Olivia

she searched it up and showed it to me

"It's the same shit on yo computer but look at it from my phone I handed it to her

she laughed "It's not even funny tho cuz I ain't never been more confused in my life" she said

"Maybe they got some confused with the news report..." she trailed off

"This nigga still ain't respond" I mugged

12:46 AM

"Ouu it fucking stank" we scrunched our noses up

we laughed and made our way to the bar

"yall got cranberry juice" I yelled to the man behind the bar

He slid me a small bottle

"How much" I asked

"On me" he said loud enough I could hear

"Thank you" I laughed

He kinda cute

I'll kinda beat yo ass I heard Zi's voice in my head

the fuck

you heard me he said

"Bitch I'm fucking Trippin" I said in Olivia's ear

"Bitch come on my feet hurt from these heels" she dragged me to a section where we could sit down

I sat down looking around at everything that was going on, parties truly weren't my environment a bitch liked to be aware of her surroundings and I can barely do that with 100+ people in a crowd

"Oh yuh this my song" Olivia said getting up

I laughed watching her swear she was eating the dance up

You needa go the fuck home Zi's deep voice boomed thru my head making me jump

Bro what the fuck did I get drugged or sum I looked at my hands to see if I was Trippin

Obeah go home now he spoke sternly

"Liv...LIV" I yelled

"what" she asked

"I think we gotta go..."I trailed off

"What you mean we just go here" she said

I squinted my eyes to make sure I wasn't trippin

"liv liv" I said in a panic

"What the fuc-" she said in confusion

"You see it too" I semi yelled making eye contact with the tall figure with dark red eye

"Come the fuck on" she pulled me towards the door

We hurried up and ran to the car

"What in the fuck type of demonic shit is going oooooon" Olivia yelled pulling out

"Bro nawl this some white people shit on god" I looked around

"Oh shit" I yelled

"What the fuck is wrong with you boutta make me fucking crash bitch"

"Bitch my whole body just had a burning sensation felt like I was on fucking fire" I touched my body

"What the fuck" she mumbled

I picked my phone up seeing Zi responded an hour ago

I scrunched my eyebrows up "He texted back" I mumbled

"What did he say" Olivia pulled into the driveway

"Stop being nosy Obeah" I read out

"Huh" she frowned

I got out of the car and went into the house I hurried to my room

To calm myself I got in the shower letting the dirt and vibes of the day wash away

2:03 AM

"Ight goodnight I love you too" Olivia closed my door

I closed my eyes drifting off to sleep

"Obeah" I heard a soft voice call out to me

I rubbed my eyes "umm who are you" I asked

"My name is OBEAH" she held her hand out

I admired her she was beautiful

"Come to me my daughter" her soft voice spoke to me

I grabbed her hand letting her lead me

I looked around seeing candles, skulls, and crystals

"My daughter" she spoke

I looked at her

"you are special and wise, no bad has come your way but it will soon..." she trailed off

"Take this you will know what to do once it arrives" she handed me a book titled The Book of Obeah

The book was old and dusty

"Wait what do you mean it will soon" I asked

"I've said enough, here" She handed me a necklace with a tiger eye pendant

"Goodbye my daughter" She placed her hand on my forehead

4:56 AM

I instantly sat up and looked around seeing I was in my room "just a dream" I mumbled

I got up about to go to the bathroom but stop one I heard something fall on the floor I flipped the light switch on to see what it was a book

The same book I had just dream

"omg omg omg" I said under my breath

I picked the book up wiping the dust off of it

I took a deep breath and then placed it on my nightstand

what typa shit is this

I grabbed my phone checked the time then went and used the bathroom

Should I go back to sleep...shii I might wake up with a fucking snake in my bed or sum

I laid back down and got comfortable

fuck it

EIGHT

July 1st

5:57 PM

"Bub imma be back to visit I promise" Me and my little brother Mari locked pinkies

"I love you sissy" he said

"I love you more" I put the rest of my bag in the trunk

I was moving into my own apartment it's all I'd been looking for and finally found one I really liked and wasted no time signing the lease

I started the car up driving to my place it was good 15 min from my mom's house which wasn't bad at all

I pulled into the complex parking and grabbing my bags I walked up to my apartment

I sighed "Move from in front of my door Ziyaan"

"Obeah can you just hear me out please I'm begging"He moved to give me the chance to unlock my door

I shook my head "Come on" I opened the door

He walked in sitting on the couch as I put my bags down in my room

"First how the fuck you find out where I live" I Sat on the table in front of him

"Ma I know it all ain't no escaping me" He spoke sternly

"Zi I ain't finna do this" I chuckled

"And what the fuck typa demonic shit you got going let me know right now" I stood up crossing my arms

He stood up

"This nice you did yo thang" He looked around

"Ziyaan" I straight-faced him

"Yes ma" He looked down at me

I squinted my eyes at him

"Ight damn well imma demon...yeah ain't nun else to it" he said nonchalantly

"What the fuck you mean..." I trailed off

I threw my arms up "Ziyaan you can't just tell me you a fucking demon nigga you look human you do everything humans can do and it's not like oh you a demon just hunting me NO NIGGA everybody can see yo ass the fuck"

"And you telling me we been out in public plenty of times and nobody recognized you as someone who died like 3 fucking years ago" I added

He sat down and then pulled me onto his lap

"Ion do everything humans do even though I do look like one but that's just how switching forms work ma and not everybody can see me it's only when I turn visible" He told me

"And shii ain't nobody recognizes me because most people simply don't know or they a demon as well" He shrugged

"So you telling me it's all these demons roaming around like everything normal " I stared at him blankly

" most of them won't be visible I don't know what it is bout you but you got sum special you able to see us even if we not visible" He said

I shook my head taking everything in

He tapped my leg signaling me to get up I got up doing a little stretch

"So when you gone leave again" I asked

"Not for another month maybe longer if I'm around you" He stood up

He grabbed my hand leading us to my room

"Aht don't sit on my bed ion know where you been" I said before he could get the chance

I took my shirt and pants leaving me in my bra in panties and I grabbed a pajama set

I looked at Zi

"Stop looking at me" I mugged him

He chuckled "Come here yo"

I walked over to him "yes" I looked up at him

He picked me up

"You look go ma" he licked his lips

"Thank you" I pecked his lips

"I missed you can I show you how much I missed you" He tugged on my panties

"yes" I bit my lip

He laid me on the bed pulling my panties down and in a circular motion he rubbed my clit causing me to let out soft moans

he went down teasing me by sucking on my clit and then pulling away

He looked up at me and we locked eye contact "You look so beautiful" he mumbled

He pinned my leg behind my head and started eating me up sloppily

My moans filled the whole apartment loud enough that my neighbor could hear

"mmm I'm gonna cum" I moaned

He kept his motion making my head fly back

"Fuuuck" I moaned cumming all over his face

I watch as he licked up all my juices then stood up looking down at me

I got up pushing him onto the bed

7:12 PM

I kept eye contact with Beah as she teased me back by licking the tip of my dick

She finally gave in stuffing most of my dick in her mouth I held her hair back as she slurped me up

"Uhh fuck" I groaned pushing her head down and causing her to gag she added two hands making my toes curl

"Beah chill" I groaned

She speed up and I started feeling like she got one up on me I pulled her on me putting us in a 69 position

I stuck my tongue in and out her hole making her moan with my dick in her mouth the vibration made my toes curl even more

I devoured her pussy flicking my tongue on her clit, licking and sucking her up not missing a spot

That nigga ah munch!~Liaa

"Zi oh fuck" she threw her head back

mmm I hummed on her pussy causing her legs to shake from the vibration

"ooh-ooh sh-" she came all in my mouth making me swallow all her juices

she rolled over looking at me with a smirk

"What" I chuckled

she started stroking my dick keeping eye contact with me

I groaned feeling my nut coming

"put it in your mouth" I demanded

She got up hungrily putting it in her mouth

I pushed her head down nutting down her throat she came up opening her mouth showing me she swallowed it all

We both laid down exhausted trying to catch our breath

9:02

"If you want me to I will eat yo ass" I shrugged

"Omg Zi you ah ass eater" she gasped

"Hell nawl but for you ill make some exceptions" I smirked

"Stop" she laughed

"What you want to eat" I asked rubbing her ass

"Ouu America best wing" She smiled

"Ight" I laughed clicking on the website

"Lemon pepper and Jamaican jerked" I asked

Lemon pepper gone bust every mf time, especially from America's best wings OOUUUU ~Liaa

She shook her head yes and I placed the order

"So how the fuck you make your Instagram only active for me" She blurted

I chuckled "I just got it like that"

She frowned grabbing my phone

"let's make a Tik Tok" she yelled tryna get up

"no sit yo ass down" i laid on top of her so she couldn't get up

"You too big Zi" She whined

"Hush" I smacked her ass

I got off her laying on my back and pulled her on top of me

NINE

July 4th

12:00 AM

"Happy birthday" Beah yelled jumping on me

"Thank you phats" I chuckled

"I got sooo much planned omg I'm so excited" She jumped up and down

"Damn you happier than me" I pulled her into my lap

"Nigga get hyped the fuck" She grabbed my phone answering it

"You don't even know who that is" I snatched my phone putting both our faces in the camera

"Yoo" I said

"Happy birthday Zi " Everybody in the gc call said

"Yall niggas ugly" I shook my head

"Hey Beah fineass" Teedo called out to her

"Hey tie-die" She waved

"What's the moves today" I asked

"Shii" Mar and Teedo scratched their head

"Whole time we can't tell you big dawg" Brando laughed

"Mmk bye dickheads" Beah hurried up and hung up

I side-eyed her causing her to laugh

"Oh yeah they bussing them bitches" I said hearing the non-stop fireworks

"Hell yeah" She grabbed my phone

"Come on" I tapped her thigh signaling her to get up

"We going to see the fireworks" she asked getting happy

"Yeah put some shorts on" I smacked her ass

I walked out of the room

I think I love that girl

I shook my head at my thought and waited till she came out

"at this point just say you wanna be like me" I laughed seeing she tried to match me

"I do I do I do-o-o" She cheesed

"Yeah imma need for you to stop watching Kenan & Kel" I shook my head opening the door

That show will forever be fye!~Liaa

We walked outside going into the parking lot

"Ouuu that one was so pretty" Beah kept her eyes on the fireworks

I grabbed my phone out of her hands and went to the camera

"Pose" I pointed the camera at her

"unt unt I look a mess" She put her head down

"Oh wait that one actually cute" She swiped through the pictures

"Hush they all cute" I pulled her into my chest

She wrapped her arms around my waist and we watched the fireworks

9:34 PM

"Oh my gosh you look so handsome" I smiled

"Watch out" He hid his smile

"Ight come on" I rushed him out

I texted all his demon friends and family to be at dinner by 10 all from his phone and then his friend gone come back to my place to drink, chill and open gifts I was hoping everything would go good

I was kind of nervous mainly because ill be sitting at a table with all demons and also imma have to talk to them and be nice

"Not me being the passenger princess" He flipped his imaginary hair

"You are so ugly oh my gosh" I laughed stopping at the red light

"You so fine you make my dick hard" We made eye contact

"Zi you know you gotta turn everything sexual" I chuckled

"My bad lemme control myself" He said

I parked in front of the casino then got out of the car

"Casino" He smirked grabbing my hand

"Unt unt we just here to eat"

He kissed his teeth

"Do it again" I said getting ready to pop him

He held the door open and I led him into the restaurant going straight to the private room

"Happy birthday" everybody yelled once we walked in

He mugged them all and shook his head

I looked up at him and gave him a death stare

"Wooow" He held his chest acting surprised

I dragged him to his seat and then took mine

"Hey Beah" Mar waved at me

"Hey Mar and Hey everybody" I waved

Everybody said their hey's and waved back then separated into conversations

"Phats" Zi mumbled

"What's wrong" I raised my eyebrow

"Nun ion know what to get" He pulled my chair closer to him

Zi was a picky eater at any other restaurant he would just get a burger or chicken tenders but this restaurant was fancy and didn't have that

"Umm you might like the alfredo or the steak " I said

"Ight" He rubbed my tight

"Order me a Cosmopolitan" I said

"Ight" He chuckled already knowing the drill

"Yall dating" A girl asked

"Yeah they is" Brando said before me or Zi could get a chance

"Damn Beah I told you to invite her" Mar scratched his head

When I was inviting people to come I facetimed mar and shared the screen so I wouldn't invite anybody Zi ain't fuck with

"Yeah..." I trailed off

"Yikes" Teedo laughed

"I'm confused" I looked at Mar and Teedo

They both looked at the ceiling trying to avoid eye contact with me

"Hello" The waiter came in greeting us

"Hi" Everybody greeted her back

"I'll be your waitress, anything you need just call me, Can I get you guys started with a drink if your ready to order you may" She said

She went around the table and everybody ordered what they wanted

10:57

"Awwe" I cooed at the baby picture of Zi that was getting passed around the table

"Awwe my ass he was bad as hell" one of his cousins said making everybody laugh

I looked over at Zi seeing he was on his phone he been checking his phone this whole dinner make me a little irritated

"Happy Birthday to you" A couple of waiters came in with a cake

I grabbed my phone recording

"Happy birthday to you" Everybody sang to Zi

I laughed watching him mug

"Make a wish" I said

He closed his eyes and then fanned the candles out with his hand

"You so lame" I laughed stoping my recording

"Ight come on time to go" Zi said getting up and everybody else

"Damn already" I grabbed Zi's hand

He lead us out of the restaurant then got into the driver's seat

I got in the car and he pulled off

suspicious

I went to grab his phone but he moved preventing me to get it

"Zi" I straight-faced him

"Chill phat" He turned into a parking lot

I scrunched my eyebrows up and watched him open the door for me

"Come on" He reached his hand out

I took it letting him lead I looked around seeing we were at meridian hill park

if you know go look it up that joint pretty asf ~Liaa

"Go head ma" He let my hands go signaling me to go up the stair

I walked up the steps reaching the top see roses, ballons and bunch of gifts

"Zi how you gone get me gifts on your birthday" I smiled turning around to face

"I got a question" He smiled

I raised my eyebrow

"Obeah Onyx will you be my girlfriend" He said shyly

"Zi yessss" I scream hugging him

He picked me up and kissed me

"This is so pretty" I looked at the view

"Zi oh shit we gotta go back to my place everybody is probably outside confused as fuck" I covered my mouth

"Why they ova there" He asked

"Cuz after your dinner we were gone chill there" I hoped down

"Mane they needa go home then" Zi huffed

"Hush and help" I picked up some of my gifts

11:45 PM

"Bruh" Zi kissed his teeth

I laughed seeing his friends from the dinner sitting in front of my door

"Stop this is so cute" I hit Zi in his chest

I unlocked the door and let everybody in

"You dead wrong fa making us wait" Mar mugged me

"It wasn't me" I put my hands up surrounding

I walked into my bedroom locking the door I undressed myself looking for something comfortable to put on

"Phat" Zi knocked on the door

"Hmm" I hummed opening the door for him

"They stress me out" He huffed walking in and locking the door behind him

"Those you friends" I went back in the closet

"Thank you" He said taking his jeans off putting on sweatpants

"No, Thank you!!" I chuckled pulling up my white romper onesie

I walked out of the closet checking my phone

"Come on I want some cake" Zi came up behind me pressing his hard piece on me

"Why you hard" I questioned him turning around touching his piece through his sweatpants

"You look good" He looked down at me

"Ight come on" I said feeling myself getting wet

I grabbed his hand leading up out the room and into the living room where everybody was at

"You got candy" Both Teedo and mar asked at the same time

"Yes" I laughed going into the kitchen bringing out a bowl of candy and chips

"Did yall watch the watcher" Warren asked

"Nawl I heard it was good" Brando said

"Hell yeah" Brandon shook his head

I grabbed the remote searching it up

"Nigga get up" I said to mar that was sitting in my spot on the couch

"My bad" he said sitting on the floor with a couple of others

Everybody got comfortable some watching the show others laughing and drinking or playing a game

TEN

July 20th

6:23 PM

"That's ah big ole ass right der!" I hyped myself up in the mirror

"You not wearing that" Zi mumbled leaning against the doorway of the bathroom

"Delusional cuz who not" I mumbled

"HUH"

"nun" I laughed running out the room

I walked into the kitchen grabbing my box of white chocolate cover Oreos and went plopping down on the couch

Them Oreos boi oh them bitches buss!! but they limited edition only come out around Christmastime~LIaa

"Where the rem-Oh my fucking gosh" I yelled jumping up on the couch

"The fuck wrong with you" ZI question running out the room

He raised his eyebrows once he saw me standing on the couch holding onto my cookies for dear life

"Get it Ziiii" I whined pointing to the table the mouse ran behind

"Mmcht get what" He kissed his teeth mugged me

"Bae it's a fucking mouse over there" I cried

"Phat chill" Zi laughed

"Get it" I yelled

I watched as Zi walked over moved the table and the mouse ran out going directly into the shoe closet

"oh my gosh" I cried

Zi laughed closing the closet trapping the mouse inside of it

"I'm leaving i cants do this it can keep the whole apartment" I huffed wiping my tears

"Dummy get yo scary ass off the fucking couch" he told me grabbing the broom

I kissed my teeth stay on the couch as he propped the front door open then open the closet, The mouse ran out not making it far because Zi swept it out making its little body fly down the stairs

My mouth hung open

"it's gone now" He said closing and locking the front door

I pouted walking back into my room

"Phat" Zi called out to me following me into the room

"Yo scary ass" He mumbled into my ear as he wrapped his hand around my waist

I rolled my eyes and removed his hands from my waist, I watched as his face quickly turned into a mug

"Ain't it time to go" I asked reaching for my phone

"We won't go no wea if youn fix yo adittude" He spoke sternly

I rolled my eyes then gave a tight-lipped smiled

"pretty ass" He mumbled

He snatched me up by my neck and aggressively kissed me

"mmm" I moaned pulling away from the kiss

"Get fucked" He chuckled letting me go

6:42 PM

"You look good" Zi complimented

I rolled my eyes and held in my smile so he would know I was still upset at the fact he made me change

"Thank you" I mumbled

He chuckled wrapping his arm around me as we step onto the escalator

I stepped off the elevator once we reached the top and smiled seeing Chanel, I wrapped my finger around the loophole of his jeans and pulled him into the store

I pulled him around the store picking up a couple of bags I thought were cute not worrying about the price

Pussy so good he gone get it for me no matter the price ahhhhh

I laughed at my thoughts and made sure not to look at him because I knew he read my mind

We walked up to the counter letting the lady ring everything up

"it that all" She asked eyeing Zi making him mug her

"Yeah" I laughed handing her Zi's card

She waited til the receipt printed out and then handed the card back and Zi took the bags

"Where we going next" He asked as I pulled him out of the store by his pants

"Footlocker" I said pulling him inside

Once we walked in we saw Zi's friends the same ones that were at his party

"Oh just fuck me huh" He spoke getting they attention

"Yaan wassup nigga" Teedo said putting his hand up so he can dap him up

Zi mugged him and slapped his hand away

"Damn see we was gone tell you but we figure you couldn't come" Mar chuckled looking at Zi and then me

I looked up at Zi who had an unamused look on his face

"Hey" The girl from the party that asked us if we were dating spoke eyeing Zi

"Sup Kenya" He said dryly looking over at the shoes

"Hii" I spoke with a big smile just to be petty cuz the bitch was damn near boutta droll over him

"Hey" She mumbled

I chuckled pulling Zi's pants indicating I was ready to go

"Ight we gone" Zi mumbled leading us out the store

"Oh there's a party going on at my place later wil-" Kenya started

"Nah" He said quickly deading the conversation

I let out a petty laugh looking at her facial expression

now look at you looking dumb as fuck

I lead the way going into the food court but quickly backed out seeing the crowd

Any other day this mall dry as fuck but okay

"I'm ready to go" I huffed pouting

"You sure" He asked grabbing my chin and lifting my head up

"Mhmm" I hummed

He leaned in giving me a sloppy kiss

"Smile pretty" He said pulling away

I quickly put on the biggest smile showing every single tooth in my mouth

"Fine ass" He tucked his bottom lip in his mouth

"Thank you baby" I blushed

He wrapped his arm around me leading up to the exit, He opened the passenger side letting me slide in and going to his side

"What you want to eat" He questioned pulling out the parking lot

"Outback" I suggested

"Ight" He nodded putting in the directions

8:23 PM

"Boy move" I giggled moving his hand

"You look so good right now my dick hard" He mumbled

"Zi" I straight-faced him

He huffed and looked at the menu

"So bae is you really a demon" I busted out looking up at him

"Beah yes" Zi grumbled

I chuckled at him now having an attitude

"Do sum demonish then cuz you seem pretty human to me" I said mugging him

I jumped feeling my body start to burn like that one time in the car

"Ziyaan" I yelped

He sat there with a smirk on his face

"Bitch ass" I mumbled mugged him

I watched as his smirk faded and turned into a mug, He crossed his arm on his chest

"Uhh" I let out a moan but quickly gasped covering my mouth

My hand gripped the table feeling vibration against my pussy

"Zi w-what is that" I asked trying not to moan

I made eye contact with him seeing his smirk appear back on his face

"Uncover yo mouth" He said sternly

I obeyed quickly removing my hand, I bit my lip trying not to let a moan escape from my lips as the vibration increased

I kept my eyes on watching as he stared at me intensely, I was shocked there was nothing on my pussy it was like he was doing the vibration with his mind

I bite down on my lip harder seeing the waiter come

"Hello what can I start you guys with" The waiter asked

"We both want pink lemonade and we ready to order our meal let me get a steak with a side of mash potatoes and she wants wings with french fries and make sure they fresh" He said all in one breath

"Okay is that a-"

"Yes bruh!" Zi dismissed her

"Fuck" I gasped once I saw her disappear

"Cum for me" He demanded increasing the vibration

I threw my head back and let out my moans not caring anymore

"Mmmm bae" I moaned as I released

I threw my head back and sighed feeling the vibration stop

"ZIyaan" I whined getting up feeling my juices drip down my leg

I watched as he smiled showcasing his pearly whites, I gave him a big mug and walked away going into the bathroom

I hurried wiping myself and took my panties off because they were drenched

"Dumbass" I said sitting back in our booth

"bet you'll mind yo business next ti-" I cut him off throwing my wet panties at his face

He took them off his face and made eye contact with me his face held an expression I couldn't read

He stuffed my panties in his pocket making me raise my eyebrows

"bae lemme eat yo pussy in front all these white people" He blurted

My jaw dropped but I quickly picked it up and licked my lips, I crossed my leg and smiled seeing the waiter bring our food

I took a bite of one of my wings and moaned at how good it was

"Lemme get one" Zi said grabbing a wing before I could get a chance to respond

My face quickly turned into a frown

"What the fuck I told you bout that shit!" I semi-yelled

10:21 PM

Location: HELL

"Don't make me beat the fuck outta you" I grumbled snatching my phone back from Kenya

"Mmcht" She kissed her teeth and rubbed my chest

"BITCH move!" I yelled

She quickly hopped up going to the other side of the couch

"Who done got you mad" Mal chuckled rolling up

I waved him off and clicked on Beah's contact

"Ziyaan" She said once the call connect

"Phat I miss you" I told her

"Where the fuck you at nigga" She grumbled

"I'm coming baby I gotta handle this shit first. ight?" I responded

"you wit a bitch cuz why yo location off" She yelled

"Pha-"

"Tell that hoe how yo whole face was just in my coochie" She cut me off

"Obeah shut the fuck up that location shit don't work down hea" I semi-yelled making everybody look at him

"Fuck you and that devil bitch" She said before hanging up

I sighed rubbing my temple

"dayumm yall niggas ugly" Satan's voice boomed through the room making me kiss my teeth

"Heyyy" Kenya dragged out batting her eyelashes at Satan

He looked at her with a disgusted face making me chuckle

"Ha take yall fuck ass files" He grumbled throwing them all at us

I kissed my teeth grabbed the file not even taking the time to look at it and walked through the door appearing back on earth

I was transported to Beah's room where I saw her asleep in her bead peacefully, I smiled taking my clothes off, and hoping in the bed cuddling her

"I hate you" she mumbled

"mm" I hummed pulling her closer to me

CPSIA information can be obtained
at www.ICGtesting.com
Printed in the USA
LVHW020632210323
742063LV00012B/1911

9 781805 099345